MR. NOISY

by Roger Hargreaves

PSS!
PRICE STERN SLOAN
An Imprint of Penguin Group (USA) Inc.

Mr. Noisy was a very, very noisy person indeed.

For example: If Mr. Noisy were reading this story to you, he'd be shouting at the top of his voice.

And the top of Mr. Noisy's voice is a very loud place.

You can hear it a hundred miles away!

For example: When most people sneeze you can hear them in the next room.

But . . . Ahhh-CHOO.

When Mr. Noisy sneezes you can hear him in the next country!

Now, this story starts with Mr. Noisy asleep in bed, in his bedroom, in his house, which is on top of a hill.

He was snoring.

And, as you can well imagine, when Mr. Noisy snores, that is a snore worth hearing.

It sounds more like a herd of running elephants than a snore!

Then Mr. Noisy's alarm clock went off.

Mr. Noisy's alarm clock sounds like no other alarm clock in the world.

It sounds more like a fire engine!

Mr. Noisy woke up.

And so too did all the people who lived in Wobbletown, which is at the bottom of Mr. Noisy's hill.

Later that day, Mr. Noisy decided that he had to go shopping.

He went out of his house, shutting the door behind him.

BANG!

The door wobbled. The house wobbled. The whole hill wobbled.

Wobbletown wobbled. Even a bird, flying high above Wobbletown, wobbled!

Then Mr. Noisy walked down the hill.

CLUMP! CLUMP! CLUMP!

He walked into the baker's shop.

CRASH! went the door as he opened it.

BANG! went the door as he shut it.

"I'D LIKE A LOAF OF BREAD," boomed Mr. Noisy to Mrs. Crumb, the baker.

Mrs. Crumb trembled, and sold him a loaf.

Then Mr. Noisy walked along the street to the butcher.

CLUMP! CLUMP! CLUMP!

He walked into the butcher's shop.

CRASH! went the door as he opened it.

BANG! went the door as he shut it.

"I'D LIKE A PIECE OF MEAT," boomed Mr. Noisy to Mr. Bacon, the butcher.

Mr. Bacon trembled, and sold him some meat.

Afterward, Mrs. Crumb met Mr. Bacon in the street.

"We really must do something about Mr. Noisy being so noisy," she said.

"Absolutely," replied Mr. Bacon. "But what?"

"I know," said Mrs. Crumb, and she whispered into Mr. Bacon's ear.

Mr. Bacon smiled a small smile, which grew into a broad grin.

"Mrs. Crumb," he said, "I think you have the answer!"

The following day Mr. Noisy again went down to Wobbletown to shop.

CLUMP! CLUMP! CLUMP!

He went into Mrs. Crumb's shop.

"I'D LIKE A LOAF OF BREAD," he boomed.

"Sorry! What did you say?" asked Mrs. Crumb, pretending not to hear.

"I'D LIKE A LOAF OF BREAD!" Mr. Noisy shouted.

"Sorry," said Mrs. Crumb, putting her hand to her ear. "Can you speak up please!"

"I'D . . . LIKE . . . A . . . LOAF . . . OF . . . BREAD!" roared Mr. Noisy.

"Can't hear you," replied Mrs. Crumb.

Mr. Noisy gave up and went out.

Mr. Noisy went into Mr. Bacon's shop.

"I'D LIKE A PIECE OF MEAT," Mr. Noisy boomed.

Mr. Bacon pretended not to notice.

"I'D LIKE A PIECE OF MEAT!" Mr. Noisy shouted.

"Did you say something?" asked Mr. Bacon.

"I . . . SAID . . . I'D . . . LIKE . . . A . . . PIECE . . . OF . . . MEAT!" roared Mr. Noisy.

"Pardon?" said Mr. Bacon.

Mr. Noisy gave up.

And went out.

And went home.

And went to bed.

Hungry!

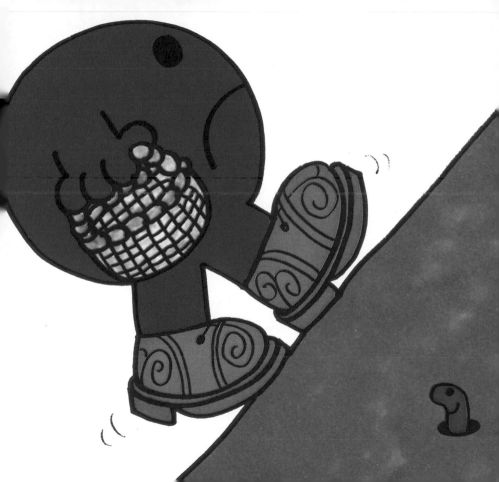

The next day Mr. Noisy tried again.

He went into Mrs. Crumb's shop.

"I'D LIKE A LOAF OF BREAD," he boomed.

"A what?" asked Mrs. Crumb.

Mr. Noisy started shouting at the very top of his voice.

"A . . . LOAF . . . OF . . . " and then he stopped. And then he thought.

And then he said quietly, "I'd like a loaf of bread please, Mrs. Crumb."

Mrs. Crumb smiled.

"Certainly," she said.

Then Mr. Noisy went into Mr. Bacon's shop.

"I'D LIKE A PIECE OF MEAT," he boomed.

"Did you say something?" asked Mr. Bacon

"YES . . . I . . . DID," shouted Mr. Noisy at the very, very top of his voice.

"I . . . SAID . . . I'D . . . LIKE . . . A . . . " and then he stopped. And then he thought.

And then he said quietly, "I'd like a piece of meat please, Mr. Bacon."

Mr. Bacon smiled.

"My pleasure," he said.

So, carrying his bread and his meat, Mr. Noisy set off for home, up the hill.

CLUMP! CLUMP! CLUMP!

Then he stopped. Then he thought. And then, do you know what he did?

He tiptoed!

A tiptoe was something Mr. Noisy had never ever tried before.

It was fun!

Mr. Noisy arrived at his front door.

He put out his hand to open the door, and then he stopped. And then he thought. And then, do you know what he did?

He opened the door—very quietly.

He stepped inside.

And then he shut the door—very gently.

Quietly and gently were two things Mr. Noisy had never tried before either.

They were fun, too!

And do you know something?

Mr. Noisy isn't as noisy as he used to be.

And do you know something else?

The people of Wobbletown are delighted—especially Mrs. Crumb and Mr. Bacon.

And do you know something else?

Mr. Noisy has even learned how to whisper!